You are a part of my heart.

Before you were born, I gave a part of my heart to Mommy.
And she gave a part to me.

When I first held you, my heart grew.

When you crawled, that made my heart happy.

When you walked, that made my heart proud.

When you jumped, my heart jumped with you.

Then you made a friend and gave away part of your heart.

When they hurt you, we were there.
You told us you'd never give your heart again.

But someday you'll find the right one to give your heart to.

And you'll have a baby heart of your own.

But even then, when you're all grown, you must know that always, always...

You are a part of my heart.

Our story:
Mike and Sansu met in wonderful Lissa Rovetch's children's book class at Pixar several years ago. They are excited to self-publish their first book and look forward to partnering with traditional publishers on future projects.

Mike Sundy
Author

Sansu
Illustrator

Mike Sundy writes children's books and screenplays in the San Francisco Bay area. He's a Notre Dame graduate and formerly worked at Pixar Animation Studios.

phastman@hotmail.com

mikesundy.blogspot.com

Sansu ("mountain water" in Korean) is a children's book author, illustrator, and animator living in the San Francisco area. She currently works as a lighting artist at Pixar Animation Studios.

hellosansu@gmail.com

www.hellosansu.com

For Nora, who is always a part of my heart - Mike

For Leo, who is my sweet heart - Sansu

Made in the USA
Monee, IL
16 January 2020